Nine Animals and the Well

James Rumford

Houghton Mifflin Company Boston 2003

For Amy Flynn, my editor

www.houghtonmifflinbooks.com

The illustrations are a collage of various Japanese papers decorated by the author and
refined with brush, pen, and pencil. The flowered paper was handmade in India.
The calligraphy was done by the author. The style of the Indian numerals was patterned
after a typeface called Rohine.

For more information on Indian numerals, see Georges Ifrah's *The Universal History of
Numbers from Prehistory to the Invention of the Computer*.

The Hindi word *jee* is a term of respect as well as endearment.

Library of Congress Cataloging-in-Publication Data

Rumford, James, 1948–
The nine animals and the well / James Rumford.
p. cm.
Summary: A fable about a group of animals which strives to bring the perfect present to the
Indian raja-king's birthday party. Discusses how the numerals we use originated in India.
ISBN 0-618-30915-2 (hardcover)
[1. Fables. 2. Numerals—Fiction. 3. Gifts—Fiction. 4. Pride and vanity—Fiction.
5. Animals—Fiction. 6. Parties—Fiction. 7. India—Fiction.]   I. Title.
PZ8.2.R86Ni 2003
[E]—dc21

2002010962

Printed in Singapore
TWP 10 9 8 7 6 5 4 3 2 1

We got our nine number signs and the zero

1 2 3 4 5 6 7 8 9 0

from the Europeans, who got them from the North Africans,

١ ٢ ٣ ۴ ۴ ٦ ٧ ٨ ٩ ٥

who got them from the Arabs,

١ ٢ ٣ ۴ ٥ ٧ ٧ ٨ ٩ ٠

who got them from the Indians of India.

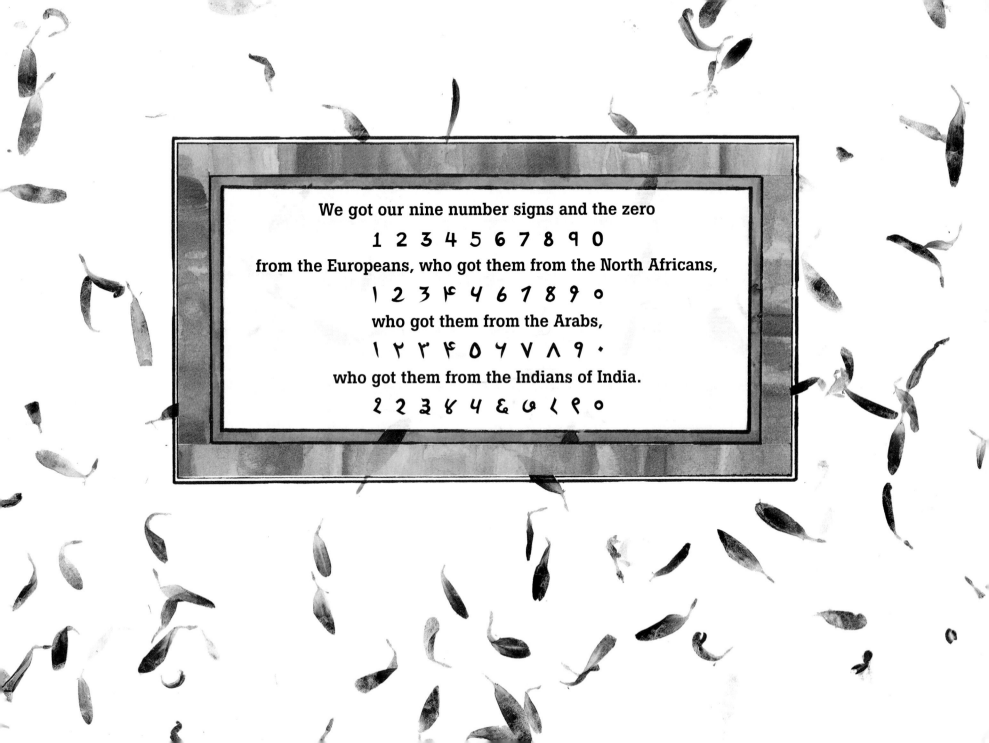

In the long-ago, rose-fragrant, animal-talking days, there lived a very young raja-king, wise beyond his years, who invited nine friends to his birthday party.

On the day of the raja-king's birthday, Monkey was the first one on the road to the palace. He jumped and skipped and trilled his tongue, so proud was he of having thought of the perfect birthday gift.

"Ho! Monkey-jee! Wait up!"

It was Rhino.

"Let's go to the party together!"

As he waited for Rhino to catch up, Monkey decided to unwrap his gift for the raja-king and show Rhino.

"No time for lunch," said Rhino when he saw the loaf of bread. "We've got to get going."

"This is not my lunch," said Monkey. "This cloudlike loaf is for the raja-king!"

The rhino tried not to snort, but he couldn't help himself. "Bread! Why, the raja-king has bakers by the dozen and as many loaves of bread as ever he could wish."

Then Rhino showed the monkey his gift: two mangoes, sun-yellow and blazoned with flames of red. "If you want, you can have one to take."

Monkey glanced at his loaf of bread, which suddenly seemed stone-heavy and rock-hard. Ashamed, he pitched it into the river, where a long-snouted gavial croc snapped it up.

"Delicious!"

Then along came Camel.

"Camel-jee!" said the monkey. "Look what we're giving the raja-king."

Like two suns, the mangoes gleamed in the camel's dark, round eyes. Camel raised her nose just a bit.

"The raja-king," she crooned, "has orchards of trees and sunny, bright mangoes whenever he wants. No, my friends, mangoes he can get. What he cannot get are these."

And she showed them three cakes, smelling summer-sweet and filled with the finest almonds Camel herself had brought from far-off Persia.

Monkey and Rhino took an embarrassed look at what now seemed like overripe mangoes.

"Not a problem," said Camel. "There's a cake for each of us."

Monkey and Rhino tossed their mangoes into the jungle, where they landed right in the mouth of a hungry dhole dog.

"Tasty!"

Just up ahead was Rabbit.

"Rabbit-jee, look what we have for the raja-king!" said Rhino.

The perfume of sweet almond cakes filled the rabbit's nostrils.

"Ah. Nice," sniffed the rabbit. "But see what you think of my gift." And he unwrapped four cones of sugar, dazzling like snowcapped peaks. "You know, we could each take a cone."

The camel, rhino, and monkey now thought so little of their three stale cakes that they tossed them to a mama mongoose and her kit.

"Lovely!"

Around the next bend, the four saw Cow.

"You should see what we're taking to the raja-king!" cried Rabbit, and he pushed the sugar under her nose.

"Oh," said the cow, feigning humility. "My gift is poor compared to this. Just flowers."

Cow then showed them her five lotus flowers, dew-fresh and glowing.

"Too bad about the sugar," said the cow.

"What do you mean?" asked the others.

"It's just that my husband spent the week hauling tons of candy sugar to the palace. The king has storerooms full."

Somehow, sugar no longer seemed a good idea. So the rabbit and camel and rhino and monkey each took a flower and chucked their four tiny, brown-colored lumps of sugar into a pile of leaves, where a queen ant and her army exclaimed, "Simply delightful!"

At the top of the next hill, the animals met Cobra.

"Halloo, Cobra-jee! See what we're taking the raja-king," cried Cow.

The glowing flowers fairly blinded Cobra. With hooded eyes, she let slip that the raja-king was *sssss*swimming in lotus.

"Better tell him," Cobra advised, "that these buds are from your own garden. You wouldn't want him to think you had poached the royal ponds.

"As for my gift, well . . . just *ssssss*ix *ssssss*pools of *ssssss*ilk ribbon."

The cow, the rabbit, the camel, the rhino, and the monkey were so taken by the grandeur of such a gift that they left their limp flowers by a

tree trunk,

where a swarm of bees

buried themselves

in the fresh pollen.

"Like honey!"

From a side road came Elephant.

"Ho! Elephant-jee," said Cobra. "Come *sssssss*ee our magnificent gift!"

The elephant peered down at the tiny rainbow of silk ribbons.

"Ah, well, if it's color you want, look at these." Out of the elephant's bag tumbled seven fire-red rubies.

A gasp of awe. The animals congratulated Elephant on her stunning gift, and she in turn mentioned something about sharing. Cobra thought it best to throw her spools of faded ribbon over a nearby cliff, where a sharp-eyed falcon snatched them up for her nest.

"Pure luxury!"

Next came Tiger, with eight black-lacquered cages on his back. In each cage was a bird bursting forth in glorious song.

"Such music!" cried Cow.

"From heaven!" enthused Rhino.

"What good are stones," said Monkey, "when the ears are so enchanted?"

Captivated by the music, the animals each took hold of a cage and let their rubies fall to the ground, where a flock of chickens swooped down on the gems, tossing them into their gullets.

What better gravel for their gizzards!

"Divine!"

Soon the animals were in sight of the palace. Just then, Peacock came rushing up, holding a sack in his beak.

"I hope I'm not late," Peacock said, then added after he saw all the cages, "You're not bringing birds, are you? Just listen."

So close were they to the palace that they could hear the chirrups and trills of a hundred songbirds.

"Best to free the poor things. But never fear. I have a gift of praise for our king."

As the peacock spoke, he ruffled out his feathers. "In this sack is a real gift. Trust me."

The other animals opened the cages and shooed the eight tuneless birds away.

By now, the peacock was strutting about, his blue tail feathers aquiver, awaiting praise and admiration.

"Gather round. Gather round, for in this sack are nine perfect gold coins, each bearing the raja-king's likeness."

"Show us, Peacock-jee! Show us!"

Peacock picked up the pouch. But as he loosened the drawstring, the gold coins spilled out and rolled down the hill. The monkey, the rhino, the camel, the rabbit—all the animals ran after the coins. But the faster they ran, the faster the coins seemed to roll until they hit a stone and flew, flashing and shining, into the air. Then down they came, like divers, into what surely was a bottomless well.

The animals ran to the well 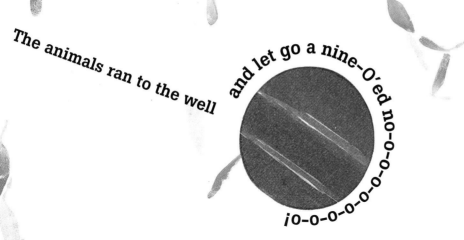 and let go a nine-O'ed no-o-o-o-o-o-o-o-o ¡O-o-o-o-o!

Monkey looked up from the edge of the deepest of wells and glared at Rhino, who snorted at Camel, who grunted at Rabbit, who twitched his nose at Cow, who mooed at Cobra, who hissed at Elephant, who trumpeted at Tiger, who roared at Peacock, who squawked, "Now what are we going to do?"

For it was true. How could they show up at the raja-king's party empty-handed or -hooved or -pawed or -mouthed or -tusked or -beaked? There arose such a squabbley bickering that it brought the raja-king out from his palace.

"Oh, my friends! You're here at last! I was afraid you weren't coming. Come in. Come in."

What could the animals do but follow the raja-king inside?

As they walked into the palace, Monkey smelled the freshly baked bread. Rhino saw a bowl of delicious mangoes. Camel spied almond cakes, Rabbit mounds of sugar, Cow lotus flowers, Cobra the silk ribbons on the raja-king's clothes, Elephant the giant ruby on his turban, Tiger the songbirds, and Peacock the gold.

In no time, though, the raja-king put his friends at ease. Soon they were eating and laughing. They even sang and danced, ending with the most amazing acrobatic trick.

"I have never enjoyed myself more," said the raja-king. "You should have come sooner."

"We would have," said the elephant, giggling, "but we had a little trouble with the gift."

"We couldn't decide," admitted the rabbit.

"You're the storyteller, Monkey-jee," said Tiger. "Make us laugh."

When the raja-king heard the story, he laughed till he cried. "What need have I of presents?" he said, catching his breath. "This story and your friendship are presents enough."

By the next day, the entire raja-kingdom knew what had happened, and, in the many rose-scented years that followed, everyone—from raja-kings to farmers, peacocks to monkeys—delighted in telling the story of the nine animals—and the well that swallowed their pride.

It was, by the way, the squiggly shapes of the Indian numbers that inspired me to make up this story, for

I saw a monkey's tail in 1, a rhino's horn in 2, camel humps in 3,

a peacock's tail feather in 9, and a deep bottomless well in 0.

I set the story in India because it was the Indians—some fifteen hundred years ago—who invented the ten curious-looking signs we use to count with.

The journey that our numbers made from India

to Arabia

to North Africa

to Europe

1 2 3 4 5 6 7 8 9 0

began in the eighth century as traders, astronomers, mathematicians, even magicians carried the ten number signs west. Even though the number signs arrived in Europe between the eleventh and thirteenth centuries, it took awhile for them to catch on. By the time they did, the Europeans were calling them "Arabic numerals," forgetting that the Arabs had gotten them from the Indians. The Arabs, by the way, call them "Indian numbers." And the Indians? They simply call them "numbers."

rabbit ears in 4, cow horns in 5, a cobra in 6, an elephant's trunk in 7, something tiger-stripe-ish in 8,